Ravenscourt
B·O·O·K·S

No Need to Shout

By

Rick Watson

Illustrated by

Linda Pierce

Columbus, OH • Chicago, IL • Redmond, WA

The McGraw·Hill Companies

SRAonline.com

 SRA

Send all inquiries to:
SRA/McGraw-Hill
8787 Orion Place
Columbus, OH 43240-4027

Printed in the United States of America.

ISBN 0-07-601589-0

2 3 4 5 6 7 8 9 MAL 08 07 06 05 04

— Chapter 1—

A Costly Experiment

"All right, class, watch closely," the science teacher said. "First we dissolve the chemicals in water." Ms. Chin wore large safety goggles and a lab coat. "Now we slowly heat the solution. What will happen next?"

Vernon slouched in the back row beside the lab closet. His black hair hung in dreadlocks. He was stuffing something into his backpack. "It'll turn red," he thought. "Anyone who read the book knows that."

Across the room by the window, Jamal yawned. He looked at his watch. Twenty minutes till the weekend. He wrote in his notebook, "It'll turn red."

Ms. Chin went on. "See? The solution is changing color. It is turning a dark red. The oxygen released by the hot water causes this to happen. In iron, this process is called rusting. In our lungs, the same kind of process turns our blood red."

"Did you say you're making blood? That's nasty!" Vernon exclaimed. "Yuck!"

A few students laughed. Some groaned. Jamal smiled and pushed his glasses higher on his nose. He liked Vernon, even if he was a loudmouth.

Ms. Chin took a deep breath. "Of course not, Vernon. Please do not disrupt the class."

"Just wait till I tell the principal about this!" shouted Vernon. He stood up beside his chair. He was very tall and skinny. "There's got to be a rule against making blood! I should go report this right now!"

"Vernon, there is no need to shout. Now, please have a seat," the teacher pleaded.

"Look, class," Vernon said in a spooky vampire voice, "she's making *blood.*"

"This is NOT blood, and you know it! Now sit down and be quiet!" Ms. Chin said sharply.

Vernon plopped down into his seat and burst into sobs. He sounded like he was really crying. "You shouldn't shout at me like that! That was so mean! Wah! Wah!"

Jamal tried not to laugh. Some of the other students tried too. But the whole class just lost it.

Ms. Chin pointed to the door. Vernon marched off to the principal's office. He grinned and winked at Jamal on his way out.

Jamal didn't understand it. He would have been ashamed to act out like that. But Vernon didn't seem to mind. He made this trip about once a week.

The students tried to settle down, but it was hard for them to pay attention. In a few minutes school would be out for the weekend. Even Ms. Chin seemed ready to go. Jamal felt sorry for her. She was new at Williams Middle School too.

The bell finally rang. Students flew out into the hall. Jamal walked to the front of the room. "Ms. Chin," he said, "do you need any help cleaning up? I know where everything goes."

"Thank you, Jamal. That would be nice," she said.

Jamal placed the Bunsen burner on the shelf. He put the jars of chemicals back into the lab closet. That's when he spotted Vernon's backpack lying there.

"Ms. Chin, looks like Vernon forgot something," he said.

"Would you mind running it up to the office?" Ms. Chin asked. "I'll finish cleaning up everything here."

"Sure."

"And, Jamal, would you ask your buddy to lay off during class? Chemistry experiments can be dangerous. It's no time for clowning around," she said as she locked the lab closet.

*"I'll see what I can do," Jamal promised as he left the room. He was glad he had helped Ms. Chin, especially after laughing like that at Vernon.

As he headed to the principal's office, Jamal thought about the weekend ahead. His mom was picking him up later. He hoped it would be a fun visit. He missed her so much.

The past year had been hard. Jamal's father had lost his job. His parents had begun to argue. Then they had split up. Jamal and his dad had moved just a few months ago. His father worked at the new paper mill in town.

Also there had been a little trouble with Jamal's grades last year. Well, a *lot* of trouble. He'd failed all but one class.

It was odd. Jamal knew the information. He just couldn't make himself finish the tests or write the papers. He had liked the experiments in science class, though. That's probably why he'd passed.

He was doing better in all his classes this year. But science class was not as much fun the second time around, even at a new school with a different teacher.

Jamal turned the corner near the office. "I thought you'd never get here," Vernon said.

"How did you get out so fast?" Jamal asked.

"I never went in," Vernon answered. "Hey, that's my backpack. You've been stealing."

"I was just bringing it to you."

"But you were also stealing. Look at this." Vernon opened his backpack. In it were two jars filled with chemicals from the lab closet.

"Hey, you'd better take those back!" Jamal whispered.

"Why should I? You walked out with them, not me," Vernon answered. "Besides, they're for a cool experiment we're doing this afternoon."

"What experiment?" Jamal asked. "What are you making now? Hey, wait! You can't take those."

"No need to shout. Ms. Chin just left, so you can't take them back," Vernon said, as he turned and headed toward the door. "You're going to really like this one. Come on, Jamal."

— Chapter 2—

Vernon's Fireworks

An hour later Vernon was at home. He stood in his kitchen looking out the window. "Why was Jamal so mad?" he asked himself. "It was just a couple of jars of chemicals. Nothing major."

But Jamal had been *very* upset. "I thought you were my friend," he had shouted. "Now Ms. Chin will think I stole those jars."

"Well, you did," Vernon had laughed, "if you think about it."

Jamal had grabbed his arm and whirled him around in the street. Vernon thought for a second that Jamal was going to punch him. He even flinched a little. It was surprising. Kids his age were usually scared of him, but not Jamal.

"That's blackmail," Jamal had said. "You'll be lucky if I don't turn you in on Monday!" And then he had stormed off on his bike.

Vernon wasn't worried about getting caught. He was used to trouble. Plus he didn't think Jamal would really tell on him. And Ms. Chin probably wouldn't notice that the jars were missing for several weeks.

Vernon looked at the instructions he had gotten from one of the high school kids. He pulled the jars out of his backpack.

"Jamal will love these homemade fireworks," he said. "I'll call him later, when they are finished."

*Meanwhile, at his house, Jamal threw some clothes into a bag. His mom would be there any minute, and he was ready to get away. He couldn't believe that Vernon had been such a jerk.

A couple of students had warned him about Vernon. They'd called him mean and stupid. But Jamal knew that Vernon wasn't stupid. He was probably smarter than most kids in his class. In fact, he was sort of a science whiz. He just didn't care about grades—or manners.

And Vernon had never seemed mean to Jamal—until today. In fact, Vernon often stood up for the smaller kids. That's how they'd met.

Some bullies had tossed peas at Jamal in the cafeteria on his* third day in school. He just sat there pretending not to notice. Soon, more and more peas landed on his table and on his head.

Just then Vernon appeared from out of nowhere. It stopped raining peas at once. "Mind if I join you?" he asked. He dropped his tray onto a pile of peas. "I'm Vernon. *Peas* to meet you."

"I'm Jamal. *Peas* have a seat." They laughed. Anything about peas became a running joke between them.

The phone rang. Jamal ran to grab it. His mom probably wanted to make sure he was ready to go.

"Hello," he answered. It was his mother on the line, but she had bad news. She had been asked to work overtime this weekend. She needed the money. She asked Jamal to wait until the next week to visit.

"It's not fair! It's not fair!" he yelled. He hung up the phone and ran out the door.

An hour later Vernon's doorbell rang. He smiled. He knew it was Jamal. No one else ever visited him. His mother sometimes rang the doorbell if she needed help carrying the grocery bags. But she wouldn't be home for another hour.

Vernon peeked at the timer on the oven. "Just one more minute. Then I turn them off," he thought. "I don't want to overheat this mixture." He went to the door and flung it open.

Instantly, dozens of sticky, wet peas splattered Vernon's face and body. They stuck in his dreadlocks. They rolled across the floor.

Jamal stood in the doorway, grinning. He was holding an empty plastic bag. "Payback, buddy. Now, how about a *peas* treaty?"

"*Peas* on Earth! By all means! Man, you are lame! Now, *peas* help me clean up this mess!"

As they wiped up the green goop, Jamal told Vernon about his mom's call. Then he told how he had been riding his bike around for the past hour. He'd stopped at the grocery store to buy some candy.

"I passed a big bag of peas in the freezer," Jamal said, scooping some peas out from under the couch. "Now we're even. But you still need to return those chemicals."

"Oh, no!" Vernon yelled. "The chemicals! I forgot all about the oven!" He ran into the kitchen.

Jamal followed right behind him. "What are you talking about?"

Vernon reached for the oven door. Jamal stepped in front of Vernon and peered into the oven. "You didn't heat any chemicals in here, did you?" Jamal reached to switch on the oven light.

Vernon yelled, "Stop!" He tried to pull Jamal's hand away, but it was too late.

A light switched on inside the oven, all right. But it was a thousand times brighter than it should have been!

Vernon felt Jamal's body slam back against him. As they were knocked to the floor, a sharp pain exploded in Vernon's ears. Then everything went silent and dark.

— Chapter 3—

The Sound of Silence

Vernon awoke in a hospital bed. The television was playing silently on the wall across the room. He saw his mother asleep in a chair.

"Mom," he tried to call. But he couldn't hear himself. He cleared his throat.

His mother woke and walked over to him. She was tall and thin, like Vernon. If her hair were in dreads like Vernon's, they would look just alike. She took Vernon's hands in hers. Then she mouthed a few words.

He asked, "What did you say, Mom?" But he couldn't hear himself. He looked at his mother's face. She was sobbing, and he couldn't hear her crying at all.

*Vernon panicked. He got his hands free and felt his ears. There were bandages on them.

"Mom, I can't hear anything!" he shouted. His mother grabbed a pen and paper. She wrote, "It's OK. You'll be fine."

"Mom, what's wrong with me?" Vernon screamed as loudly as he could. The words vibrated in his chest. They stung his throat. But he still could not hear them.

The door burst open. Two nurses came running to his bed. Vernon was startled. He hadn't heard them coming. "Help me!" he cried. "Help me!"

His mother hugged him as he cried. One nurse held his arm as the other nurse gave him a shot to calm him down. Vernon cried himself to sleep.*

Vernon dreamed about music. His favorite band played on the radio. He danced down the hallway at school. Then he played air guitar in Ms. Chin's science class. He looked around for Jamal. His friend's chair was empty.

Vernon tried to say something, but he couldn't form the words. The band played a sad, slow song like a funeral march. Vernon turned around. He was standing in an empty field. He saw a big hole like a grave. Vernon peered down into it. His backpack lay at the bottom. As he reached for it, he tumbled into the hole. He kept falling and falling. He tried to scream, but now there was no sound at all.

When Vernon woke up again, the room was dark. "Mom? Mom, are you here?" A light flickered on. The brightness hurt his eyes. It reminded him of the oven exploding.

His mother stood beside the bed. She made a circle with her thumb and first finger. "Are you okay?" she mouthed. He made the okay sign back to her.

He asked, "Is Jamal okay?" He couldn't tell how loudly he was talking.

His mother took a deep breath and looked away.

Vernon felt his heart pumping. "Is he alive?"

His mother nodded yes. Then she took a pad and pen off the desk. She wrote, "He was badly hurt. He's in a coma. But the doctors are hopeful."

Vernon leaned back and stared at the window. His mother wrote again. He read the note. "It's not your fault. The teacher told me how Jamal stole those chemicals after class."

Vernon shook his head no. This wasn't right. He wanted to tell his mom what really happened. He opened his mouth.

But he couldn't do it. Not now. He couldn't bear to talk. He couldn't bear to think. Vernon had never felt so guilty in his life.

Chapter 4

Going to Greenley

As Vernon began to recover, he started to worry about going back to school. He didn't know how he'd face everyone, especially Jamal and Ms. Chin.

He knew it would be hard, being deaf and all. What would kids think? How would they treat him? Then he found out that his mother might send him to a boarding school for hearing-impaired students. It was in a town about an hour away. That made his old school seem much better.

Vernon wrote his mother a long letter. He asked to stay with her. He promised he would study harder. He would stay out of trouble. He would take sign language classes with her after school so they could communicate better.

His mother showed the letter to the counselor at Vernon's old school. The counselor was impressed. But the doctors said that Vernon would not regain his hearing and that he should learn to sign. The best way for him to learn was to be surrounded by other people who signed well. He needed to live with other deaf students for a while.

His mother was torn. She didn't want Vernon to go away. He was all she had since her husband had died.

Finally she made a hard choice. She wrote Vernon a letter and let him read it after dinner the next evening. The letter said that Vernon had to live at the boarding school for at least a year. After that they would decide if he could move home.

"If Dad were alive, he wouldn't send me away," Vernon thought. The old Vernon would have shouted his anger, but there was no need to shout. His mother was hurting enough already. He got up from the table and went to his room.

Two days later Vernon's mother told him that Jamal had awakened from the coma. He'd been unconscious for nearly a month. Jamal could not speak or walk. The doctors said he would need therapy for several months to fully recover.

Vernon had gone to see Jamal in the hospital a couple of times while Jamal was still in the coma. Jamal didn't look too bad. He just had a bandage over his forehead.

Vernon could not look Jamal's parents in the eyes during the visits. He knew they blamed him for what had happened, and he blamed himself too. He never stayed at the hospital long.

Vernon was happy when his mom told him that Jamal was awake. But something else began to worry him. Everyone still thought Jamal had stolen the chemicals from school.

What would Jamal say when he could talk? Vernon knew he should write a letter to take the blame and to clear Jamal's name. But it seemed to be too late. Vernon felt bad about how he had acted in Ms. Chin's class. How could he tell her what he did?

Vernon thought about visiting Jamal after he woke up. He decided it would be too hard to face Jamal. He wasn't even sure Jamal would want to see him.

"Maybe going away to school is the best thing for me after all," he said.

*The next night Vernon and his mom packed his bags. She gave him several books—two about sign language and one about getting used to sudden deafness. He hadn't opened any of them. Vernon watched her place them in the backpack where he'd hidden the jars of chemicals before.

At the bus station the next morning, Vernon's mom gave him a note. It said she would write often. She asked him to do the same. He looked at her and nodded yes. They both wondered if he really would.

A few minutes later he noticed several people staring at him from across the station. At first he thought it was his hair. Then he saw his mother talking to the* bus driver. She pointed back to Vernon.

"That's great! Just tell the whole world!" Vernon shouted. "Now everyone knows your son's a deaf freak!"

His mother ran over and tried to apologize, but he wouldn't even look at her.

Vernon climbed onto the bus and turned away from the window. The other passengers could hear him crying, but he only felt the tears.

When the bus stopped an hour later, the driver walked back and looked at Vernon. He pointed out the window. A bald man wearing thick glasses stood outside. He held a sign with Vernon's name on it.

The bald man smiled and waved when Vernon stepped off the bus. He signed some words that Vernon didn't understand. Then he pointed to his car.

After Vernon placed his bags in the trunk, the man handed him a card. It said his name was Martin and that he was a counselor at Greenley School for the Deaf.

When Martin turned up the car radio, Vernon felt a surprising jolt. The whole car vibrated with a steady pulse. He couldn't really hear the music, but he could feel the beat. Vernon thought he recognized the song. Martin was rocking out! Vernon smiled and gave him a nod.

When they reached the campus, students of all ages were hanging around, visiting, and playing games. Vernon noticed them all signing to one another. Some signed gracefully, and some signed wildly. Vernon wondered about the difference. He thought it might be like whispering and shouting.

"Wow," he thought, "quiet or loud, they all sign fast." Vernon knew many of the kids had used sign language their entire lives. How would he ever catch up?

Word spread that a new student had arrived. A lot of kids came to watch as Vernon carried his bags inside. A few waved or signed to him. One was a cute girl about his age. She smiled and signed, "Hi. My name is Amy." Vernon didn't know what she'd said. He just nodded.

Vernon did know one thing. He had a lot to learn.

— Chapter 5—

Good Signs

Vernon expected the classes at Greenley to be tough. He was right about that. He took classes each day to learn sign language. That was hard enough, but his teachers expected him to keep up with his normal schoolwork as well.

Vernon learned to read his textbook before each class. This made following the class easier. Some of his teachers gave handouts or wrote notes on the board. That helped too.

Vernon kept up his grades, but even after a couple of months he still couldn't follow signed lectures or classroom discussions. Their hands were all moving too fast.

Even after he could sign better, Vernon hardly ever risked signing in class. Sometimes he had to answer a teacher's question. Some students laughed or rolled their eyes when he made mistakes. It made him think of how Ms. Chin must have felt.

Amy was in several of his classes. She never laughed at him when he messed up. He found out she was on the basketball team. Vernon started going to the games just to watch her play. She always smiled at him in the stands.

"Maybe I'll try out for the boys team next year," he thought, though he'd never played basketball before.

But what Vernon really wanted was to say something to Amy. He wanted to sign something funny, to make her laugh in a good way. Sometimes when he was alone, he would practice signing jokes or telling silly stories. But he couldn't get up the nerve to do it in public.

Vernon had expected tough class work at Greenley, but he had no idea how hard dormitory life would be. He had never lived with other kids, and he was used to doing what he wanted.

At Greenley, all the boys lived in large rooms with 10 or 12 other boys. Many of them were older, and some were mean.

The older boys ran the dormitory. Everyone had cleaning chores assigned to them, but the older boys forced the younger ones to do their chores too. It didn't seem like a good idea to tell them no.

*One night Vernon lay awake in the dark. His mother wrote him with news about Jamal. His rehabilitation was finished, and Jamal was returning to school. Vernon had not written to Jamal even once. He wondered what he would say if he did.

Just then he saw a movement across the room. Vernon lay very still and pretended to be asleep. Several of the older boys headed down the dark hall. They all looked around to make sure no one followed them.

Vernon wondered what they were up to. He sneaked toward the storeroom. He smelled smoke coming from the room, and a dim light shone under the door. Suddenly the door flew open, and Vernon was yanked inside. He* felt punches on his head and arms. Someone pushed him against the wall and held him there.

Vernon tried to yell for help. He could see the other boys grinning in the smoky air. Evan, the biggest bully in the school, signed to him, "No need to shout. No one can hear you anyway." The boys' faces all broke into laughter.

Evan signed very, very slowly. It was the same as calling Vernon stupid. "If you tell on us, we'll break you in half! Now, get out of here, dummy!" The boys all punched him again. Then they pushed him out into the hallway.

Vernon lay awake in his bed the rest of the night. There was no way he would rat on those boys. They hadn't hurt him. He couldn't understand why they were so mean. He hadn't done anything to them.

Vernon felt very alone. He had no one to talk to. He decided he had to make some friends. He would work harder on his signing skills. He wouldn't worry about making mistakes. He would sign and sign and sign. He'd be big and loud and funny, just like he used to be. He'd become his old self again. Only this time he wouldn't do stupid tricks. He wouldn't steal either.

"No," he thought, "I'll be better than I used to be. I hurt a good friend. It's time to grow up."

Vernon promised then that he would write a letter to Jamal the next day— even if he didn't want to. He would apologize and ask for forgiveness. He would write to Jamal's parents and to Ms. Chin and confess everything. It was time to come clean.

— Chapter 6—

Peas on Earth

Time passed. Vernon sent his letters but heard nothing back from his friend Jamal or the others. A few months later Vernon stood on the playground surrounded by a group of students. They laughed and clapped. One boy stomped his feet and held his side. Vernon signed rapidly. He moved his hands quickly and made funny faces. His funny stories made him popular. He was like a stand-up comic.

Just as he finished telling his joke, Amy walked up. "I must have missed a good one," she signed.

Vernon smiled and replied, "Don't worry. I'll tell it again."

Amy answered, "You can tell me at dinner. Right now you have a visitor waiting in the reception room."

Vernon was surprised. His mother had visited just a few days before. He couldn't imagine who else it could be.

"It's your friend Jamal, from back home, the one you told me about," Amy said.

"It can't be. I wrote to him months ago, and he never answered my letter."

"Maybe he's answering it now," Amy said. "Go on. He's waiting. Good luck."

Vernon's heart was racing. Sending the letter to Jamal was the hardest thing he'd ever done. But not getting an answer was even worse. Now he didn't know what to think.

Vernon walked into the reception room. Jamal sat there alone. He looked different. He was taller and thinner, and he wasn't wearing glasses. A scar about two inches long ran along one temple.

To Vernon's surprise, Jamal very slowly signed, "What took you so long?"

Vernon smiled and signed back, "How did you learn to sign?"

Jamal waved his hands and then signed, "Slow down!"

Vernon repeated the sentence very, very slowly. He thought, "This must be how people talked to me when I got here. But it's really cool that he bothered to learn."

The two friends said things they'd needed to say for almost a year. Vernon repeated his thoughts from the letter. He asked Jamal to forgive him.

*Jamal said he thought Vernon would visit him when he came out of the coma. But Vernon had left town without a word.

Jamal had been angry. He started taking signing lessons during his rehabilitation. He wanted to tell Vernon what a jerk he was when he saw him. But when he got Vernon's letter, he sensed that Vernon was trying to change. Jamal's anger slowly grew less. He wanted to be friends again. He handed Vernon a letter from Ms. Chin to read later.

Soon the talk turned to some lighter things. "What happened to your hair?" Jamal asked. "No more dreadlocks."

Vernon blushed. "My friend Amy thought that it might look cool this way, with cornrows," he said.*

"I met Amy in the office," Jamal signed. "I think she likes you."

"No, no, no. We're just friends," Vernon answered. But then he asked, "Do you really think she likes me?"

They both laughed. "I'm getting hungry," said Jamal, rubbing his belly. "Do you think we could get some food before my dad comes back for me?"

"Sure. Dinner will be ready in the cafeteria in a few minutes," Vernon said. "Come on. I'd like you to meet some of my friends. Oh, I hope you won't mind, but Amy usually sits with me and my friends at dinner."

"That doesn't surprise me at all," Jamal signed. They laughed as they started walking toward the cafeteria. "Hey! Do you know what I'd really like for dinner?"

Vernon smiled at his friend. Then he said out loud, "Yes, I do. Peas!"